20 Colourful People of Wales

resilient
strong
happy
passionate
marvellous confident special
safe
incredible
talented brave
awesome
beautiful fair
amazing
positive healthy
proud
cool inspirational
respectful
important
equal

20 Colourful People of Wales

Natalie Jones

Artwork by Telor Gwyn

You will be following the QR codes
in this book at your own risk.
We are not responsible for the
website that the QR codes lead to.

First impression: 2024
© Natalie Jones & Y Lolfa Cyf., 2024
Illustrations © Telor Gwyn
Design: Richard Huw Pritchard
Cover design: Richard Huw Pritchard

This book is subject to copyright and may not be reproduced by any means except for review purpose without the prior written consent of the publishers.

The publishers wish to acknowledge the support of
the Books Council of Wales.

ISBN: 978-1-80099-613-7

Published and printed in Wales on paper
from well-maintained forests by
Y Lolfa Cyf., Talybont, Ceredigion SY24 5HE
e-mail ylolfa@ylolfa.com
website www.ylolfa.com
tel. 01970 832 304

Introduction

Hello!

I'm Natalie Jones! I am a mother of Jamaican descent. I have a degree in psychology, and I'm a teacher. I'm also lucky that I've had the opportunity to work as a presenter on S4C and contribute to several factual programmes. I also worked with the Welsh **Government** and other organisations to create anti-racism resources for children.

Unfortunately there aren't many Black and Asian teachers in Welsh schools and therefore the minority children of our communities don't have many **role models** to support and **inspire** them. But the intention of this book is to show how AMAZINGLY TALENTED the Black and Asian people of Wales are and that EVERY child should be PROUD of their **identity**. Hopefully the book will motivate children to follow their dreams and remind them of how important it is to look after each other and be kind.

Enjoy!

Natalie

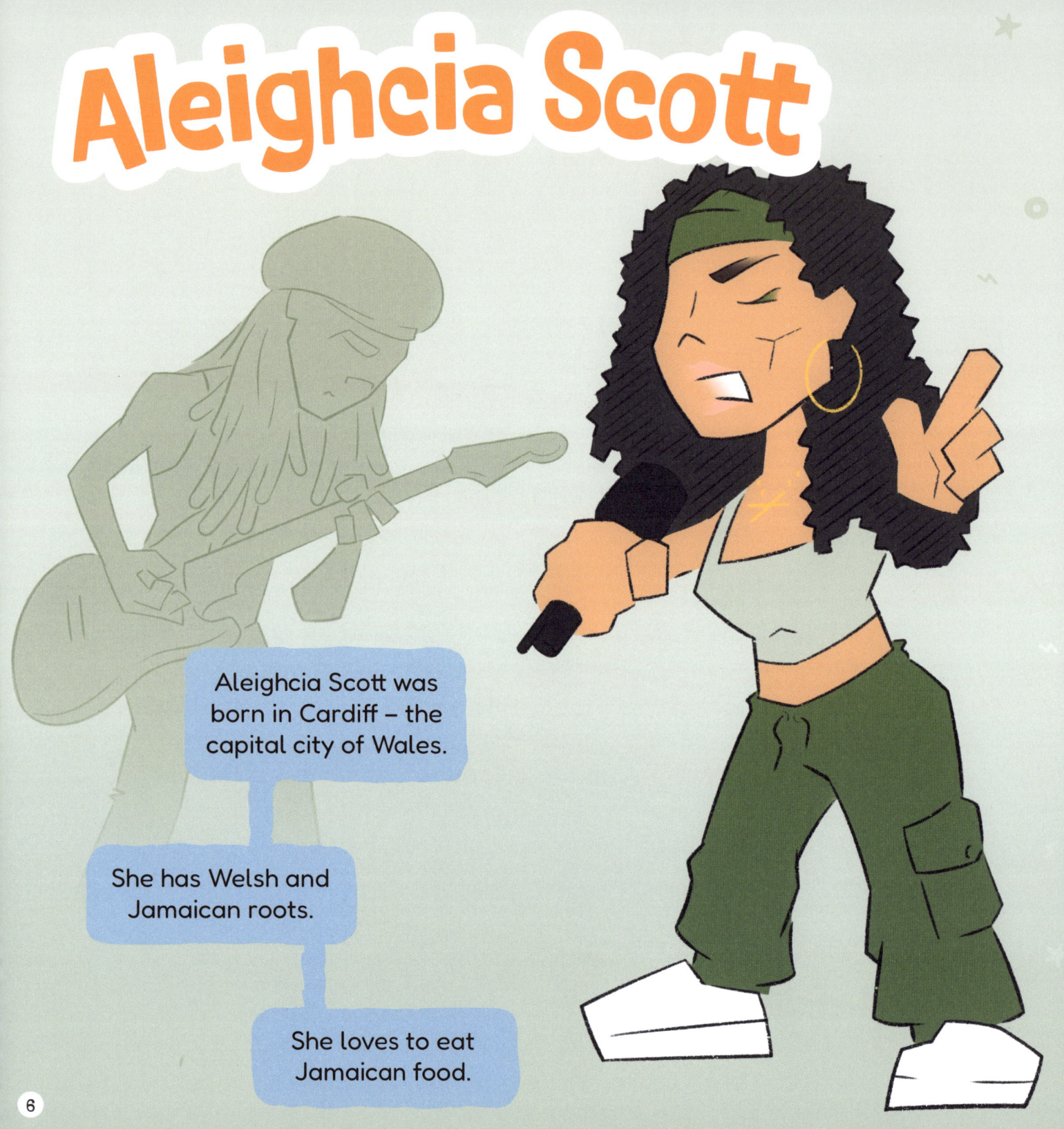

When she grew up, she decided to learn to speak and sing in Welsh. This is very important to her.

Aleighcia loves a special kind of music called reggae. Reggae music first started in Jamaica. It's the kind of music that makes you want to dance and sing along!

She has released two albums – *Forever In Love* in 2018 and *Windrush Baby* in 2023.

Aleighcia has made a **career** out of singing. She travels and performs all around Britain, Jamaica and online. She's also a presenter for BBC Radio Wales and BBC Radio 1Xtra.

Did you know?

Aleighcia has been chosen as one of the judges on the Welsh singing programme *Y Llais* (The Voice).

Check out Aleighcia's great song here!

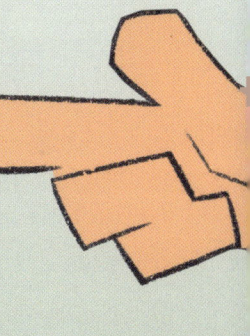

Penny Dinh

Penny Dinh lives in Cardiff and has Vietnamese **heritage**.

She is a researcher at Cardiff University.

In an important study, Penny found out that there aren't many teachers with different skin colours in Wales. This means that some children don't have teachers who look like them. Because of Penny's study, schools can now do their best to find new teachers from all **races**.

Penny is working really hard to make Wales a fair and happy place for all children and teachers, whatever their skin colour.

Treating someone differently because of their skin colour is not okay. This is called racism.

Penny is a **role model** because she fights for what's right in a positive way and makes other people realise they can do the same.

Who is your role model or superhero?

Emily Pemberton

Emily Pemberton was born in Cardiff.

She is Welsh and Jamaican.

She's proud of being able to speak Welsh and thinks that *Cymraeg* is cool!

Emily has presented on television. She worked on a programme called *Pawb a'i Farn: Black Lives Matter*, which won a BAFTA award. She also presented a programme called *Windrush: Rhwng Dau Fyd*, which told the story of Caribbean people moving to Britain.

It's really important to her that we get rid of racism in Wales and that we all have opportunities to do whatever we want to do, whether we speak English or Welsh. This is called equality.

Emily also works with **Urdd Gobaith Cymru** to make sure that the young people of Wales get the support they need to succeed and that Wales is a better, fairer country.

Did you know?

The Urdd has a mascot called Mistar Urdd who has his own song: 'Hei Mistar Urdd'. The song broke two Guinness World Records in 2022 – for the most uploaded videos of people singing the same song on Facebook and Twitter/X in one hour.

Sing along with Mistar Urdd!

11

Dr Phillip Moore

Dr Phillip Moore was born on a Caribbean island called Barbados.

He is a **surgeon** in Bangor. To become a surgeon, Phillip had to study and practise for seven years.

He wanted to make patients feel comfortable when they weren't very well so he decided to learn Welsh. Now he can speak to them in their first language.

Learning and speaking Welsh has helped him to show his respect for his patients and to feel part of the community.

He's been on the television programme *Ward Plant* (*Children's Ward*) on S4C.

Phillip shows that being brave enough to learn something new can make your life *and* other people's lives better.

Phillip won an award at the National **Eisteddfod** for learning Welsh. He is just as proud of this as he is of becoming a surgeon.

What are you most proud of?

Melanie Owen

Melanie Owen is from Aberystwyth.

She is Welsh and Jamaican.

She's very talented and has won many awards. She is a farmer, comedian, presenter, writer and actor. What a busy person!

As a child, she enjoyed performing in front of her family – singing, dancing or playing an instrument. When she was in Year 3 at school, she had a funny part in the Christmas show. She enjoyed making people laugh and after that she jumped at every opportunity to perform.

One day, she met a famous actor called Hugh Jackman and accidentally ate his croissant! But he was very nice about it and didn't get mad at her.

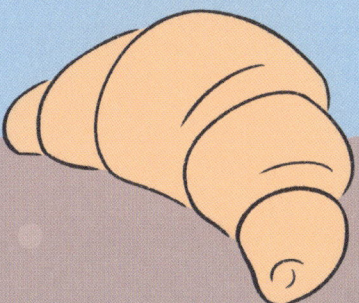

Melanie enjoys being on television and radio. She also loves animals and working on her family farm.

She uses her skills and energy to make the world a better and happier place, especially for children. If she sees children being treated unfairly, she speaks up to make things better.

Did you know?

Laughing is good for your heart and your lungs!

Mali Ann Rees

Mali Ann Rees is an actor from Cardiff.

She is Welsh and Jamaican. Speaking two languages – Welsh and English – has helped her to achieve her dream of becoming an actor.

Mali has acted in the theatre, in television dramas and in movies! She loves her job because it means that she can entertain people and make them happy.

Mali believes that it's important to talk about our feelings and what makes us different – as well as the things that we all have in common.

When she was a little girl, she didn't see any Welsh actors who looked like her. So she became one herself! She believes that all children should have good role models and does her best to be one.

Mali is thoughtful because she cares about the future of all children.

How can you show kindness?

Sunil Patel

Sunil Patel was born in India but now lives in Cardiff.

He's a dad, a businessman and a trainer who loves football. He volunteers at his local football and cricket clubs.

When he was a little boy, his parents brought him to Wales. Some children said nasty things about the colour of his skin. This racism made Sunil feel upset. He decided that when he grew up, he would do something about it – and that's exactly what he's done!

Sunil became one of the first people to work with a **charity** called Show Racism the Red Card. This charity visits children all over Britain to teach them how to treat each other with respect.

Now Sunil runs a business that trains people to treat staff fairly at work. His job is very important because it helps everyone feel confident and safe.

Sunil is wonderful because he works hard to stop children from experiencing the same kind of racism as he did.

Did you know?

Every October, Show Racism the Red Card has a Wear Red Day. You can celebrate this important day by learning about racism and raising money for the charity. And by wearing something red!

Mirain Iwerydd

Mirain Iwerydd from Crymych is a television and radio presenter.

She hosts fun radio shows on BBC Radio Cymru and BBC Radio Cymru 2. Every Sunday morning she plays great music and helps make Sundays happy for everyone!

Mirain also presents a Welsh television show for children called *Sêr Steilio* (*Styling the Stars*) and a show for families called *Heno* (*Tonight*).

S4C

Mirain also won a public speaking award when she was younger with the Urdd! Since then, she's kept on learning and working hard to be the best presenter she can.

When she's not busy presenting, she loves sewing. She has a lot of colourful clothes.

She has been to a music festival in the Netherlands and interviewed lots of pop stars. She has even hosted a show about politics for children.

She's very passionate about helping people, and she visits schools to share stories and talk to as many children as she can.

What a talented person!

Who would you like to interview?

Richard Parks

Richard Parks is an explorer from Pontypridd!

He has Welsh and Jamaican heritage.

He loved science so he went to university to study to be a dentist.

He was also an amazing rugby player and played for Wales! But after some injuries, he knew he had to change his career again – so he became an explorer!

Richard has travelled to many faraway places and even climbed to the very top of Mount Everest!

He's so brave and fit that he has broken many world records. He is the first person of colour to reach the South Pole and he has skied all by himself in Antarctica. This needs resilience, which means never giving up! Richard teaches us that if we try our best, we become strong.

Guess what else Richard does? He makes films about his adventures and talks about how we can take care of our planet.

Did you know?

Mount Everest is the tallest mountain in the world! It's eight times higher than Yr Wyddfa (Snowdon)!

Rabbi Matondo

Rabbi Matondo was born in Liverpool, but when he was only two years old, his family packed up their things and moved to Cardiff.

His parents were born in the Congo in Central Africa.

He is a famous footballer who has played for Wales since he was eighteen.

When he was young, Rabbi loved playing football on the streets with his family and friends.

One day, some important people from Cardiff City football club noticed how good Rabbi was at playing football. They asked him if he wanted to join their team and learn even more about the game. Rabbi was over the moon!

Rabbi could have played football for England or the Congo – but he chose Wales!

After a while, the famous football club, Manchester City, saw how amazing Rabbi was at football. They asked him to come and play for their team, and Rabbi couldn't believe it!

Did you know?

The Welsh national anthem, 'Hen Wlad Fy Nhadau' is sung before every football match by players and supporters to show their love for Wales.

The best national anthem in the world!

Nooh Omar Ibrahim

Nooh Omar is from Butetown in Cardiff.

He has family roots in Somalia and Wales.

He offers regular fitness sessions for his community to help everybody stay active and healthy.

He noticed that children in his area didn't have many fun things to do after school. So he and a friend called Saeed Abdi worked hard to find a safe place for young people to meet and play together. Then he made sure they could play the games they wanted and had snacks to eat too!

He loves to make young people happy. His goal is to make all children stars – not only in sports but also in life.

Guess what? In 2022, he was chosen as one of eight finalists in the BBC **Unsung Hero** Sports Personality of the Year award. That's a really big deal!

Nooh also works with the Urdd, to give everyone the chance to play rugby.

He won 'Young Learner of the Year' in the 2024 Urdd National Eisteddfod, only a year and a half after starting to learn Welsh.

Nooh uses his imagination and skills to make the lives of other young people better.

What would make children happy where you live?

Lloyd Lewis

Lloyd Lewis from Newport is a presenter on S4C's *Stwnsh*, a Welsh rugby player and a rapper.

He has Welsh and Jamaican heritage.

He studied hard at university to learn about media and English literature.

Lloyd has played rugby for Pontypool, Newport and for Wales – he can run very fast!

Lloyd also believes that it's important children have fun and are treated fairly.

Music has always been important to Lloyd. He's known for rapping in Welsh and English. He strongly believes that children should get to hear rap music in Welsh. That's why he wrote and performed the song, 'Pwy Sy'n Galw?' ('Who's Calling?') with his friend Dom James.

Lloyd is fantastic because he reminds us how cool and fun the Welsh language is.

If you were a rapper, what would you rap about?

Molara Awen

Molara Awen, was born in England but now lives in Pembrokeshire.

Her mum is English and her dad is Nigerian.

She has travelled the world singing all kinds of music – soul, reggae, pop and folk. She also teaches people how to sing!

Molara has two children who have helped her learn Welsh. Now she can sing lots of songs in more than five languages! She sings in English, Welsh, French, Yoruba and Spanish. That's impressive!

Sadly Molara's cousin died because of unfairness and racism. Since then, she has worked extra hard to stop this happening to anyone else. She even helped the British **government** make a new law called Seni's Law.

Molara and her family have starred in *Gogglebocs* (*Gogglebox*) on S4C.

Molara opens her home to children and their families to teach them about the amazing things that Black and Brown people have done.

Can you say 'Hello' in the five languages Molara speaks?

Hello (English)
Helô (Welsh)
Bonjour (French)
Pẹlẹ o (Yoruba)
Hola (Spanish)

Margaret Ogunbanwo

Margaret Ogunbanwo was born in Lagos, in the African country of Nigeria. Margaret and her husband decided to move to the UK after getting married.

She now lives in Caernarfon and has learned Welsh.

She is the mother of two children – one is the rapper Sage Todz!

Margaret has lots of positive energy!

She is an amazing chef. She loves to cook and write about food from all over the world. This includes Nigerian, Caribbean, Indian, Italian, Mediterranean, Balinese, Syrian and Latino foods.

Margaret is also a businesswoman. She sells special spice blends and sauces that she has made herself. They're very tasty! She helps other people to run new businesses too.

Margaret was very brave moving from her country. But she has found happiness and success in Wales.

Imagine how nice it would be to eat dinner at Margaret's house!

What's your favourite meal?

Ify Iwobi

Ify Iwobi is a **musician** from Swansea.

She is Welsh and Nigerian.

Ify is a fantastic piano player. She loves music!

Ify has performed in Wales, London and America. She has appeared on television, on the radio and on stage. And she's won lots of awards for her talent and hard work.

The most amazing thing about Ify is how hard she works to make other people happy. Especially children! In Nigeria, families must pay to send their children to school. She has paid for many Nigerian children to go to school when their families could not afford it.

Ify also helps other young people who love music to find their voices – and instruments!

That's not all! In 2021, Ify wrote a very cool song with her friends to raise money for the NHS. The song is called 'We Won't Forget'.

If you were in Ify's band, which instrument would you like to play?

Drums ◯   Guitar ◯   Trumpet ◯

Piano ◯   Tambourine ◯

Relax by listening to one of Ify's songs.

Joseff Gnagbo

Joseff Gnagbo was born in West Africa, in a country called Ivory Coast, but he now lives in Cardiff.

He is a teacher, a translator and a **carer**.

Since he was little, Joseff has always enjoyed learning languages. He first spoke French, then he learned Swahili, Italian, Russian, German and Arabic!

But then something awful happened. There was a war in Ivory Coast and Joseff had to leave his home and find a safe place to live. He became a **refugee**. It was a very hard and frightening time for him and his family.

After some time, Joseff's family was told they could move to Wales. He decided to learn Welsh right away. This is the seventh language that he has learned.

Now he helps other people learn Welsh and he's the chairman of the Welsh Language Society, Cymdeithas yr Iaith.

Joseff also works hard to make sure that everyone in Wales is treated fairly and can speak Welsh whenever they want. This is called activism!

Did you know?

The Welsh language is famous because one village in Wales has a very long name — the second longest in the world: Llanfairpwllgwyngyllgogerychwyrndrobwll-llantysiliogogogoch!

Nelly Adam

Nelly Adams was born in London and has family from Kenya in Africa. She now lives in Cardiff.

Nelly works in a hospital and is also a poet.

She's been in the news, on television and on the radio talking about why we should treat one another fairly and how we can all be better friends to each other.

Nelly does her best to work for peace in Palestine. She also raises money for people who live in countries that have been affected by war.

Nelly teaches people about the racism that's still happening around the world and how to stop it. Sometimes she even uses poetry to explain it!

'Let's get together and raise money for the needy,
Put your hands in your pockets and don't be greedy!
Because even a penny will help build the pot,
So that we can give Palestine the entire lot!'

Nelly has another cool name – it's 'Queen Niche'!

If you had a nickname, what would it be?

Ali Abdi

He loves his community and football.

Ali Abdi is from Grangetown in Cardiff.

His family is Welsh and connected to Somaliland in East Africa.

Ali is really special because he's won awards for helping young people – like Cardiff University's Professional Excellence Rising Star Award! Sometimes he even gives awards to other people who do amazing things!

He thinks it's very important for people to work together to make good things happen.

He wants to make sure that all children get the most out of school and find the best jobs when they grow up. But, above all it's important to him that children are happy, confident and that they enjoy themselves!

He helps people who can't speak English or Welsh to be part of the community.

Did you know?

More than 94 languages are spoken in Cardiff!

Malachy Edwards

Malachy was born in London but now lives on the Welsh island, Ynys Môn.

He writes a column in the Welsh magazine *Golwg*. He writes about different things – from politics to films.

Malachy released *Y Delyn Aur* in 2023, which is an autobiography. An autobiography is a book about your own life. In the book, he talks about his family history, race and religion. His family comes from Ireland, Wales and Barbados.

In his spare time, he likes to help others. He supports people to write their own books and tell their own stories.

Malachy Edwards is special because he helps other people love their language and **identity**.

What do you love about Wales and the Welsh language?

Malachy studied law for six years and his job now is looking after people in the workplace. He makes sure that everybody is treated fairly, is getting a good wage and that the working conditions are safe.

Sheldon Mills

Sheldon Mills is a lawyer from Cardiff who was brought up by his proud nan.

Sheldon started going on walks and holding events to raise money for charity with his family when he was a child. Doing good things in the community has always been important to him.

He decided that he wanted to study law at King's College, London, when he was still at school. One teacher told him that he would never go there. But Sheldon was **determined**, and he worked very hard and made his dream come true.

He also works hard to make sure that the LGBTQIA+ community is treated fairly. Standing up for other people is extremely important to him.

Sheldon helps people to get funds to develop **inventions**! How cool is that?!

Once he visited a Welsh community in South America. He loved having Welsh culture in common with the people there. He says that even though he works in London now, he loves coming back home to Wales.

Did you know?

There are many Welsh speakers living in South America today in a region called Patagonia. Their families moved from Wales over 150 years ago to protect their Welsh language and find better lives. The journey took two months on a ship called *Mimosa*.

Glossary

career – making a living out of doing something

carer – someone who looks after a family member, partner or friend who needs help because of illness

charity – charities help people who are in need, for example because they are ill, poor or have no home

determined – wanting to do something very much and not allowing anything to stop you

eisteddfod - a Welsh festival with many competitions such as music and poetry

government – the group of people who run the country

heritage – things that are handed down or your background

identity – what makes you who you are

inspire – to give someone an exciting idea about what to do or create

invention – a clever device or tool

musician – someone who creates or performs music

race – a group of people who share the same history, culture and appearance

refugee – someone who must leave their country because it's unsafe

role model – someone you look up to as a good example

surgeon – a doctor who performs operations

unsung hero – someone who does great things without praise

Urdd Gobaith Cymru – an organisation which provides experiences for children and young people through the medium of Welsh

Activities

1 Draw three lines to show what these people like.

    Aleighcia Scott   Making people laugh

    Malachy Edwards   Reggae music

    Melanie Owen   Writing

2 Name three things that Richard Parks has done.

----

3 Which football teams has Rabbi Matondo played for? Tick three answers.

    Wales ◯   Manchester City ◯

    England ◯   Cardiff City ◯

4 Tick which sentences are true and which are false.

	True	False
Joseff Gnagbo hated learning languages when he was little.		
In Nigeria, children go to school for free.		
Margaret Ogunbanwo lives in south Wales.		

5 Find the jobs in the wordsearch.

t	r	a	n	s	l	a	t	o	r
e	s	u	r	g	e	o	n	a	d
a	e	b	f	l	s	g	c	n	p
c	m	i	a	a	u	t	h	o	r
h	c	h	c	o	r	d	e	y	k
e	o	r	t	s	g	z	f	u	s
r	s	c	o	m	e	d	i	a	n
v	y	x	r	w	o	y	d	k	x
p	r	e	s	e	n	t	e	r	z

chef   surgeon   teacher   author
translator   presenter   comedian   actor

6 Colour in the pictures.

7 Which languages are in the tables?
Complete the name of the language.

cath
car
bara
ysgol
llyfr
W....................

cat
car
bread
school
book
E....................

chat
voiture
pain
école
livre
F....................

gato
auto
pan
escuela
libro
S....................

ologbo
ọkọ ayọkẹlẹ
akara
ile-iwe
iwe
Y....................

8 Can you label the compass?

north   south   east   west

9 Richard Parks is on an adventure. Which route takes him to the top of the mountain?

10 List everything that you're proud of:

-
-
-
-
-
-
-
-
-
-
-

resilient
strong
happy
passionate
marvellous confident special
safe
incredible
talented brave
awesome
beautiful fair
amazing
positive healthy
proud
cool inspirational
respectful
important
equal

Also by Y Lolfa

£20 (Pack of 5 books)

THE FISH PRINCESS

North Wales Africa Society
& Casia Wiliam

y Olfa

£5.99

£6.99

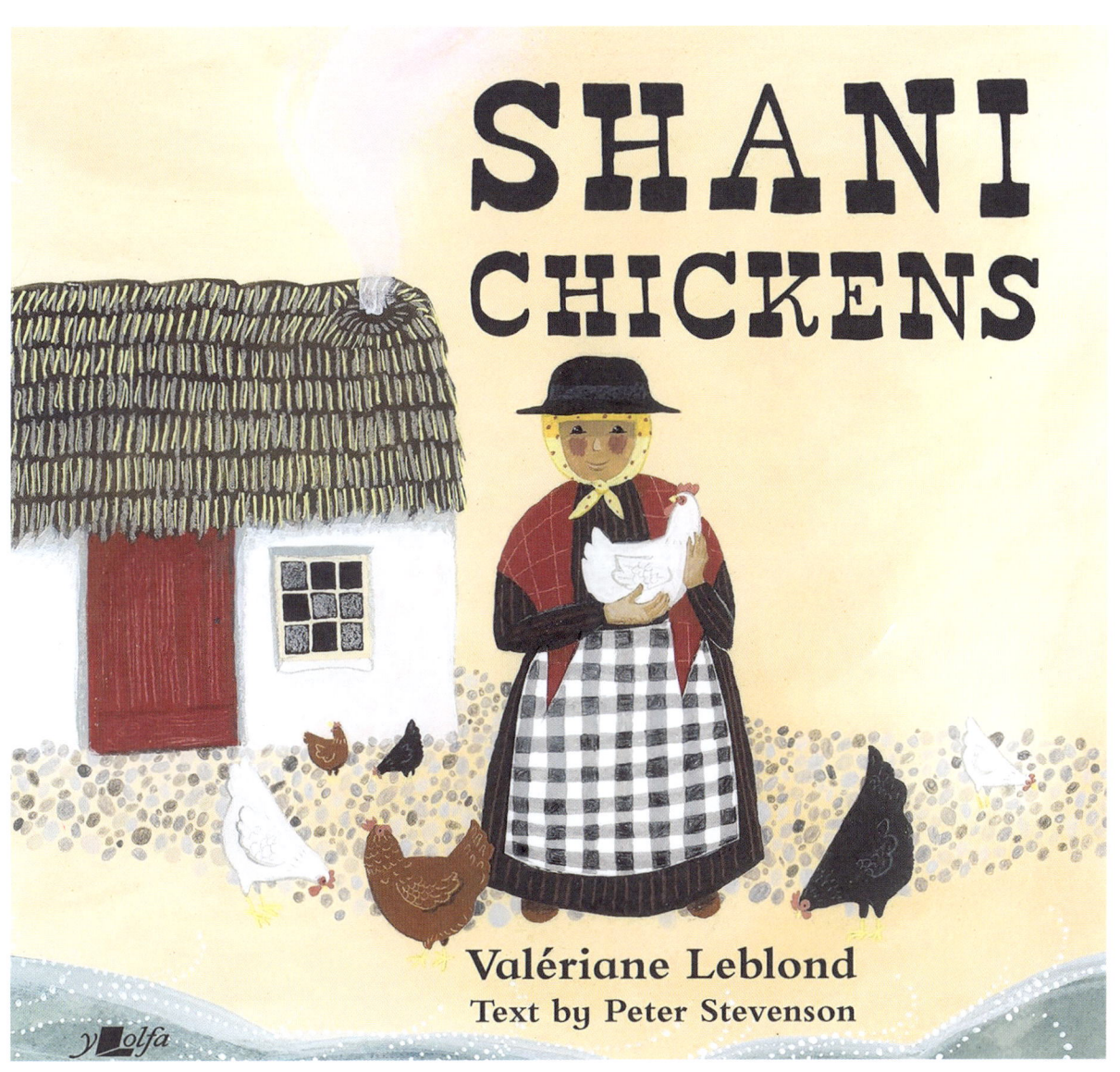

£7.99